The Veterinarian Fashion Designer

WRITTEN BY NADINE A. LUKE
ILLUSTRATED BY LARAIB FATIMA

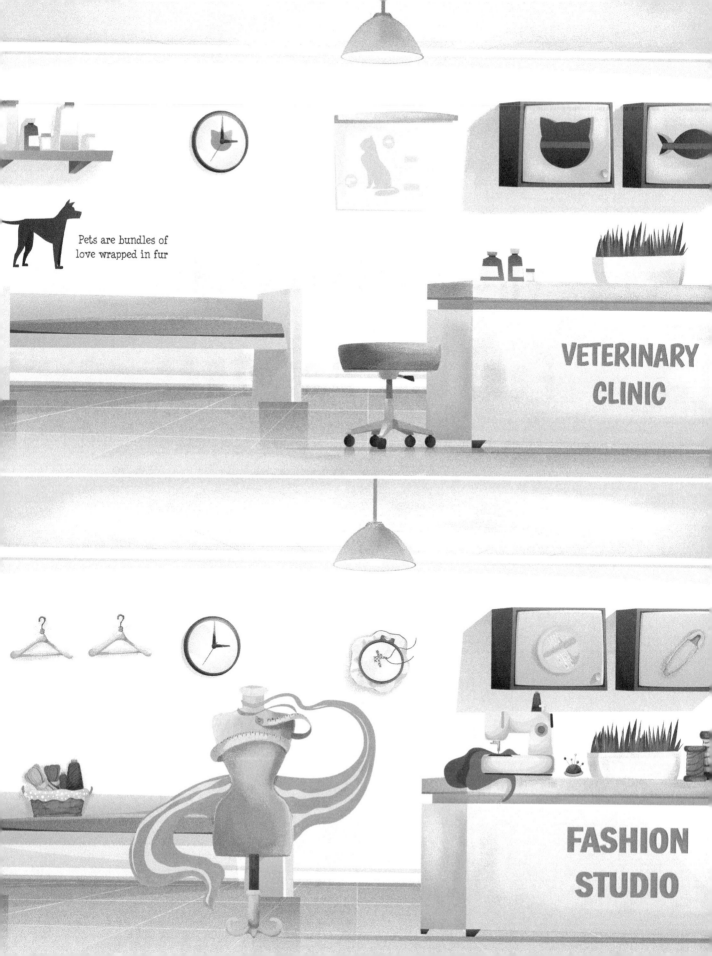

Pets are bundles of love wrapped in fur

VETERINARY CLINIC

FASHION STUDIO

ISBN:978-1-7350635-0-8 (Paperback)
ISBN: 978-1-7350635-1-5 (Hardcover)

DEDICATION

THIS BOOK IS DEDICATED TO MY DAUGHTER TIARA, MY CROWN OF GLORY, DESTINED TO SUCCEED, AND TO ALL OF THE CHILDREN WHO DARE TO FOLLOW THEIR DREAMS.

I am a veterinarian and a fashion designer!
Yes, you heard me right.

I am five years old and I already know that I'm going to help a lot of animals and people.

My mommy and daddy agree because they said, "Tiara, don't worry about what people say. You can be the World's Greatest Veterinarian and a Fashion Designer if that's what you want to be!"

I love all animals, even insects. I can spend hours watching a pile of ants march from the dirt to a bug and back to the dirt.

It's amazing how they stay in a straight line no matter where they go.

If they were in my class, my teacher would love them!

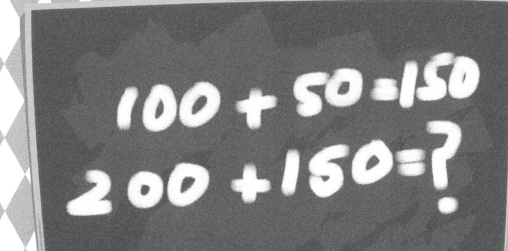

Maybe if she brought the ants to class they could teach us how to stay in a straight line.

Sometimes I put my finger down so one can walk on my hand. It usually tickles as it walks up my arm.

Then I carefully lower my hand and return the ant to its family so it can go home.

My favorite animals are dogs. I have two poodles named Shorty and Pinky. I take good care of them.

I make sure they have water, food and go for walks in the backyard every day.

Since I am an animal doctor, they are usually my patients. I wrap their foot whenever it gets broken.

They are not very good patients because they always tear their bandages off.

We play games like fetch and hide and seek.

I think hide and seek is Shorty's favorite! He's really good at it too because when it's his turn to hide I can never find him.

I look everywhere, behind the tree, under the bush and behind the garage, but I can't find him anywhere!

When I finally give up and go inside, all of a sudden, he shows up!

I know that I am a fashion designer because one day it was really cold outside and I had to take Shorty for a walk.

As soon as we went outside, he ran back into the house.

Then it hit me. I had on a jacket. He needed one too.

So, I went inside and told my mom that Shorty needed a jacket because it was too cold outside. She looked at me kind of strange.

I asked if I could use an old sweater to make him a jacket and she said, "Yes."

My mom helped me cut out the parts. I wanted to do it all by myself but I couldn't because I was too little to use the big scissors.

"Turn here, cut a hole there, add a button here, pull here, cut there." I told her. My mom is a wonderful Designer's Assistant.

Once we were done, Shorty and Pinky had the best-looking outfits any dog could have.

I can't wait until I am able to make clothes for people too!

After all, I am not just a veterinarian who likes to help animals. . .

I am the World's Greatest Fashion Designer for everyone, including animals!

CPSIA information can be obtained
at www.ICGtesting.com
Printed in the USA
BVHW010807020720
582733BV00021B/1

9 781735 063515